THE WORLD OF BEATRIX POTTER · PETER RABBIT ™

# The Tale of
# Benjamin Bunny

FREDERICK WARNE
Published by the Penguin Group
Penguin Books Ltd., 80 Strand, London WC2R oRL, England
Penguin Group (USA) Inc., 375 Hudson Street, New York, New York 10014, USA
Penguin Group (Australia), 250 Camberwell Road,
Camberwell, Victoria 3124, Australia (a division of Pearson Australia Group Pty. Ltd.)
Penguin Group (Canada), 90 Eglinton Avenue East, Suite 700, Toronto,
Ontario M4P 2Y3, Canada (a division of Pearson Penguin Canada Inc.)
Penguin Books India Pvt. Ltd., 11 Community Centre,
Panchsheel Park, New Delhi 110 017, India
Penguin Group (NZ), 67 Apollo Drive, Rosedale, Auckland 0632,
New Zealand (a division of Pearson New Zealand Ltd.)
Penguin Books (South Africa) (Pty.)
Ltd, 24 Sturdee Avenue, Rosebank, Johannesburg 2196, South Africa

Penguin Books Ltd., Registered Offices: 80 Strand, London WC2R oRL, England

www.peterrabbit.com

001 - 10 9 8 7 6 5 4 3 2 1

This edition copyright © Frederick Warne & Co., 2012
Frederick Warne & Co. is the owner of all rights, copyrights and
trademarks in the Beatrix Potter character names and illustrations.

With thanks to Ruth Palmer.
Manufactured in China.

ISBN 978-0-7232-6836-9

# The Tale of
# Benjamin Bunny

based on the original tale by

## BEATRIX POTTER™

F. WARNE & CO

An Imprint of Penguin Group (USA) Inc.

One morning, a little rabbit sat on a bank.
He pricked up his ears and listened to the *trit-trot,
trit-trot* of a pony.

A buggy was coming along the road. It was
driven by Mr. McGregor, and beside him sat
Mrs. McGregor in her best bonnet.

As soon as they had passed, little Benjamin
Bunny slid down into the road and set off with
a hop, skip, and a jump to visit his relatives.
They lived in the woods behind Mr. McGregor's
garden.

These woods were full of rabbit holes, and in the neatest, sandiest hole of all lived Benjamin's aunt and his cousins—Flopsy, Mopsy, Cottontail, and Peter.

Old Mrs. Rabbit was a widow. She earned her living by knitting rabbit-wool mittens and muffs. She also sold herbs and rosemary tea and lavender.

Little Benjamin did not really want to see his aunt. He went around the back of the fir tree, where he nearly tumbled on top of his cousin Peter.

Peter was sitting by himself. He looked ill and was dressed in a red cotton handkerchief.

"Peter," whispered little Benjamin. "Who has your clothes?"

Peter replied, "The scarecrow in Mr. McGregor's garden."

He told Benjamin how he had been chased around the garden and had dropped his shoes and coat.

Little Benjamin sat down beside his cousin and told him that Mr. McGregor had gone out in a buggy, and Mrs. McGregor, too; and certainly for the whole day, because she was wearing her best bonnet.

Peter said he hoped that it would rain on her bonnet.

Just then, old Mrs. Rabbit's voice was heard inside the rabbit hole, calling, "Cottontail! Cottontail! Fetch some more chamomile tea for Peter!"

Peter said he thought he might feel better if he went for a walk.

They went away, hand in hand, and jumped upon the wall at the end of the woods. From there, they looked down into Mr. McGregor's garden. Peter's coat and shoes were plainly seen upon the scarecrow, topped with an old tam-o'-shanter cap of Mr. McGregor's.

Little Benjamin said, "It spoils people's clothes to squeeze under the gate. The proper way to get in is to climb down the pear tree."

Peter fell down headfirst, but it didn't matter since the garden bed below was newly raked and quite soft. It had been planted with lettuce.

They left many odd little footprints all over the bed, especially little Benjamin, who was wearing clogs.

Little Benjamin said that the first thing to do was to get back Peter's clothes so they could use the handkerchief.

They took them off the scarecrow. It had rained during the night; there was water in the shoes, and the coat had shrunk somewhat.

Benjamin tried on the tam-o'-shanter, but it was too big for him.

Then he suggested that they fill the handkerchief with onions as a little present for his aunt.

Peter did not seem to be enjoying himself. He kept hearing noises.

Benjamin, on the other hand, was perfectly at home and ate a lettuce leaf. He said that he was in the habit of coming to the garden with his father to get lettuce for their Sunday dinner. (The name of little Benjamin's papa was old Mr. Benjamin Bunny.)

The lettuce was very good.

Peter did not eat anything; he said he would like to go home. Soon, he dropped half the onions.

Little Benjamin said that it was not possible to get back up the pear tree with the onions. He boldly led the way toward the other end of the garden. They went along a little plank walkway, under a sunny, redbrick wall.

The mice sat on their doorsteps cracking cherry pits and winked at Peter Rabbit and little Benjamin Bunny.

They went among flowerpots and frames and tubs. Peter heard noises worse than ever, and his eyes were as big as lollipops!

He was a step or two in front of his cousin when he suddenly stopped.

This is what those little rabbits saw around that corner!

Little Benjamin took one look, and in no time he hid himself and Peter and the onions underneath a large basket.

The cat got up and stretched and came and sniffed the basket. Perhaps she liked the smell of onions!

Anyway, she sat down on top of the basket.

She sat there for *five hours*.

Under the basket it was quite dark, and the smell of onions was awful; it made Peter Rabbit and little Benjamin cry.

The sun went behind the woods, and it was now quite late in the afternoon. But still the cat sat upon the basket.

Finally there was a *pitter-patter, pitter-patter,* and some bits of mortar fell from the wall above.

The cat looked up and saw old Mr. Benjamin Bunny prancing along the top of the wall.

He was smoking a pipe and had a little switch in his hand.

He was looking for his son.

Old Mr. Bunny had no opinion whatsoever of cats. He took a tremendous jump off the top of the wall onto the cat and knocked it off the basket, kicking it into the greenhouse, scratching off a handful of fur.

The cat was much too surprised to scratch back.

When old Mr. Bunny had driven the cat into the greenhouse, he locked the door.

Then he came back to the basket and took out
his son Benjamin by the ears and spanked him
with the little switch.

Then he took out his nephew Peter.

Then he took out the handkerchief of onions
and marched out of the garden.

When Mr. McGregor returned about half an hour later, he saw several things that puzzled him.

It looked as though some person had been walking all over the garden in a pair of clogs— only the footprints were too ridiculously little!

Also he could not understand how the cat had managed to shut herself up *inside* the greenhouse, locking the door from the *outside*.

When Peter got home, his mother forgave him because she was so glad to see that he had found his shoes and coat. Cottontail and Peter folded up the handkerchief, and old Mrs. Rabbit strung up the onions and hung them from the kitchen ceiling with the bunches of herbs and the lavender.